Walker Books is grateful for permission to reproduce the following:

"I Talk with the Moon" originally appeared in *Instructor*, May 1985. Reprinted by permission of the author who controls all rights.

"Wake Up" from *Mud, Moon and Me* by Zaro Weil, first published in the UK by Orchard Books Franklin Watts, a division of the Watts Publishing Group, 96 Leonard Street, London EC2A 4RH.

"Morning Song" from *Poems for Small Friends* by Bobbi Katz; copyright © Random House, Inc. 1989; reproduced by permission of the author.

Acknowledgements

Each story in this collection has been previously published by Walker Books
as a self-contained volume, except:

First published 1998 by Walker Books Ltd, 87 Vauxhall Walk, London SE11 5HJ

Text © year of publication individual authors
Illustrations © year of publication individual illustrators
Main cover illustration © 1998 Helen Oxenbury
All other cover illustrations taken from the books represented in this treasury

10 9 8 7 6 5 4 3 2 1

Printed in Belgium

British Library Cataloguing in Publication Data
A catalogue record for this book is available from the British Library.

ISBN 0-7445-6140-X

MY BUSY
BOOK

WALKER BOOKS
AND SUBSIDIARIES
LONDON • BOSTON • SYDNEY

Contents

WAKING UP

TIME

Poems from

A CUP OF — STARSHINE

edited by Jill Bennett
illustrated by Graham Percy

I TALK WITH THE MOON

I talk with the moon, said the owl
While she lingers over my tree
I talk with the moon, said the owl
And the night belongs to me.

I talk with the sun, said the wren
As soon as he starts to shine
I talk with the sun, said the wren
And the day is mine.

Beverly McLoughland

WAKE UP

Wake up

Morning
Has
Galloped
Bareback
All night to
Get here

Zaro Weil

MORNING SONG

Today is a day to catch tadpoles.
Today is a day to explore.
Today is a day to get started.
Come on! Let's not sleep any more.

Outside the sunbeams are dancing.
The leaves sing a rustling song.
Today is a day for adventures,
And I hope that you'll come along!

Bobbi Katz

WET WORLD

by Norma Simon illustrated by Alexi Natchev

A wet world waited
when I woke up this morning,
wet windows, wet trees,
wet leaves, wet grass,
wet street, wet rooftops,
wet world.

A warm breakfast waited
when I went down the stairs,
warm toast, warm cereal,
warm cocoa,
warm tummy.

A stiff raincoat slipped on my stiff arms.
Stiff red boots over my wiggly toes.
Hat, coat, boots.
Out to the
wet world.

I walk on the wet world.
Wet mud tugs my boots.
Wet pavement splashes my boots.
Wet rain sprinkles my hat.
Wet rain drips down my coat.
Wet cars swish down my road.
Windscreen wipers wipe the wet.
Whish, whish, whish, whish.
Whish away the wet.

Wet puddles cover wet boots.
Dry feet in wet boots.
Dry arms in wet coat.
Dry head in wet hat.
Dry me,
wet world.

A warm world waited when I went home,
warm mother, warm father,
warm stove.

A wet world waited outside my window.
A warm bed waited inside my room.
A warm kiss kissed me.
And now I'm in bed.
I wonder what world
will wait in the morning.

Good night,
wet world.

WHAT ARE MORNINGS LIKE?

by Catherine and Laurence Anholt

Mum and Dad are fast asleep

And all the house is quiet.

 I slip into baby's room

And start a little riot.

TIME

TO BE

NOISY

We're the noisy dinosaurs, *crash, bang, wallop!*
We're the noisy dinosaurs, *crash, bang, wallop!*
If you're sleeping, we'll wake you up!
We're the noisy dinosaurs, *crash, bang, wallop!*

We're the hungry dinosaurs, *um, um, um!*
We're the hungry dinosaurs, *um, um, um!*
We want eggs with jam on top!
We're the hungry dinosaurs, *um, um, um!*

We're the busy dinosaurs, *play, play, play!*
We're the busy dinosaurs, *play, play, play!*
We've got toys to share with you!
We're the busy dinosaurs, *play, play, play!*

We're the happy dinosaurs, *ha, ha, ha!*
We're the happy dinosaurs, *ha, ha, ha!*
We tell jokes and tickle each other!
We're the happy dinosaurs, *ha, ha, ha!*

We're the dancing dinosaurs, *quick, quick, slow!*
We're the dancing dinosaurs,
quick, quick, slow!
Hold our hands but don't step
on our feet!
We're the dancing dinosaurs,
quick, quick, slow!

DINOSAURS!

BY JOHN WATSON

We're the thirsty dinosaurs, *slurp, slurp, glug!*
We're the thirsty dinosaurs, *slurp, slurp, glug!*
We'll drink the sea and your bathwater too!
We're the thirsty dinosaurs, *slurp, slurp, glug!*

CRASH!

We're the angry dinosaurs, *roar, roar, roar!*
We're the angry dinosaurs, *roar, roar, roar!*
Get out of our way or we'll eat you up!
We're the angry dinosaurs, *roar, roar, roar!*

We're the naughty dinosaurs, *bad, bad, bad!*
We're the naughty dinosaurs, *bad, bad, bad!*
We say sorry and promise to be good!
We're the naughty dinosaurs, *bad, bad, bad!*

We're the quiet dinosaurs, *shh, shh, shh!*
We're the quiet dinosaurs, *shh, shh, shh!*
We read books and play hide-and-seek!
We're the quiet dinosaurs, *shh, shh, shh!*

We're the dirty dinosaurs, *scrub, scrub, scrub!*
We're the dirty dinosaurs, *scrub, scrub, scrub!*
We wash our necks and brush our teeth!
We're the dirty dinosaurs, *scrub, scrub, scrub!*

We're the sleepy dinosaurs, *yawn, yawn, yawn!*
We're the sleepy dinosaurs, *yawn, yawn, yawn!*
Send us to bed with a great big kiss!
We're the sleepy dinosaurs,
yawn, yawn, yawn!

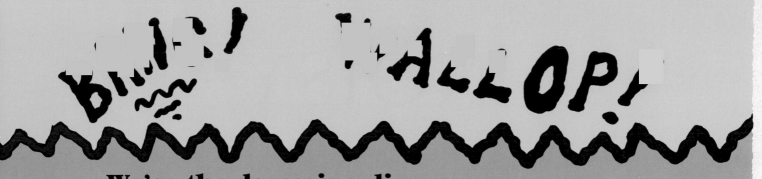

BANG! WALLOP!

We're the dreaming dinosaurs,
snore, snore, snore!
We're the dreaming dinosaurs,
snore,
snore,
snore!

We dream of monsters
and children too!
We're the dreaming dinosaurs,
snore, snore,
snore!

NOISY

Noisy noises!

Pan lids clashing,

Dog barking,

Plate smashing,

Telephone ringing,

Baby bawling,

Midnight cats

Cat-a-wauling,

Door slamming,

Aeroplane zooming,

Vacuum cleaner

Vroom-vroom-vrooming,

And if I dance and sing a tune,

Baby joins in with a saucepan and spoon.

by Shirley Hughes

Gentle noises...

Dry leaves swishing,

Falling rain

Splashing, splishing,

Rustling trees

Hardly stirring,

Lazy cat

Softly purring.

Story's over,

Bedtime's come,

Crooning baby

Sucks his thumb.

All quiet, not a peep,

Everyone is fast asleep.

Animal Sounds

by Louise Voce

baaaa

neigh

woof

cluck

squeak

miaow

mooo

oink

TIME TO
PLAY

WHAT IF?

I went into the
garden with Grump.
We played "What if?"

"What if I sneezed,"
I said to Grump,
"and all the worms
came up and
sneezed too?"

"That would be funny,"
said Grump.

"What if I danced,"
I said to Grump,
"and all the mice
came out and
danced with me?"

"That would be
funny," said Grump.

BY JOYCE DUNBAR

"What if I whistled," I said, "and all the birds flew down and whistled too?"

"You can't whistle," said Grump.

"I know I can't," I said, "But I'll be able to whistle one day ... and then you never know *what* might happen."

I'm a Jolly Farmer

I'm a jolly farmer,
Here's my
horse and cart.

Giddy up, horsy!
It's time to
make a start.

by Julie Lacome

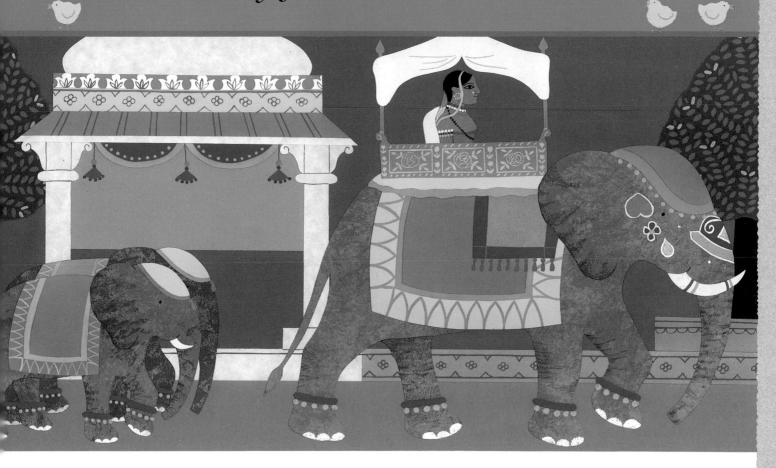

I'm a smiling princess,
An elephant I ride.

My throne is perched
on top of him –
I'm glad his
back's so wide!

27

I'm a wildlife warden,
I've tracked this
   lion here.

He looks as though
   he's fast asleep
But I won't
   get too near!

I'm a deep sea diver,
I've met a
    dolphin friend.

We swim an
    underwater race –
She beats me
    in the end.

I'm Little Red
   Riding Hood,
My granny's
   ill in bed.

"What big teeth
   you have!" I say.
I wish I hadn't
   come today ...

I wish I'd stayed
   at home to play ...

With Fred!

TIME TO
COOK

LITTLE MOUSE MAKES SWEETS

by Michelle Cartlidge

Sweetmaker Mouse is expecting a special visitor today. Little Mouse is coming to her sweetshop to learn how to make sweets.

Little Mouse is very excited. "Look at all the different sweets in the

window!" he says. "Let's go inside now please, Mummy."

"Today we're going to make peppermint creams and chocolate fudge," says Sweetmaker Mouse. "But first we must wash our hands."

"Oh, they're my favourite sweets. Can we make peppermint creams first? What do we need?" cries Little Mouse.

PEPPERMINT CREAMS

large & small bowl	*lemon squeezer*	*teaspoon*	*sieve*

 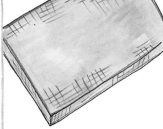 

wooden spoon	*fork*	*wooden board*	*knife*

450 gm icing sugar	*egg white*	*half a lemon*	*peppermint flavouring*

Sweetmaker Mouse tells Little Mouse what to do.

"Put the icing sugar in the sieve and sift it into the large bowl to get the lumps out. Do a little bit at a time.

"Now I'll separate the egg yolk from the white into the small bowl.

"You can whisk the egg white with the fork. We don't need the yolk.

34

"Add the whisked egg white to the bowl of icing sugar and mix it with the wooden spoon. Mix in 1 teaspoon of peppermint flavouring.

"Squeeze the lemon and slowly add the juice until the mixture is not too sticky. Now you can roll it into a ball with your hands.

"Sprinkle some icing sugar onto the wooden board and some on your hands too. Roll the mixture on the board into long sausages about 2 cm thick," says Sweetmaker Mouse.

"Cut the rolls into slices 5 mm thick. Leave them in a cool place until they set."

"Let's make the fudge while we wait," says Little Mouse. "What do we need?"

CHOCOLATE FUDGE

saucepan half full of hot water

sieve

tablespoon

wooden spoon

large & small bowl

knife & teaspoon

baking tray

50 gm butter

100 gm plain chocolate

4 tablespoons single cream

1 teaspoon vanilla flavouring

450 gm icing sugar

Little Mouse breaks up the chocolate and puts it in the small bowl with the butter. Sweetmaker Mouse stirs the mixture over the saucepan of hot water until it has melted. Then she takes the bowl out of the saucepan.

Sweetmaker Mouse says, "Stir in 1 teaspoon of vanilla flavouring and 4 tablespoons of cream.

"Sift the icing sugar and slowly mix it into the small bowl. If the bowl gets too full, put the mixture in the large bowl.

"Now you can grease the tin with the paper from the butter. Put the mixture in and press it down with the spoon. Leave it to set in the fridge and cut it into squares with the knife."

Little Mouse's father comes to collect him. "Look, Daddy," he says. "I've made enough sweets for you and Mummy, my little sister and all my friends, and there are some for me too!"

COOK

by Paul Manning
illustrated by Nicola Bayley

Who's that
in the big
white
hat?

Sticky
paste,
try a taste.

What shall
we make –
a chocolate
cake?

Cook looking,
how's it
cooking?

Three, four...
a spoonful
more.

Bang, bong,
sound the
gong.

Slop, splatter,
mix the
batter.

What's for tea?
Look
and see!

RHYME
TIME

Sing a song of sixpence,
A pocket full of rye;
Four and twenty blackbirds
    Baked in a pie.
When the pie was opened,
    The birds began to sing;
Wasn't that a dainty dish
    To set before the king?

40

Humpty Dumpty sat on a wall,

Humpty Dumpty had a great fall.

All the king's horses and all the king's men

Couldn't put Humpty together again.

One, two,
Buckle my shoe;

Three, four,
Knock at the door;

Five, six,
Pick up sticks;

Seven, eight,
Lay them straight;

Nine, ten,
A big fat hen;

MY SHOE

illustrated by
Charlotte Voake

Eleven, twelve,
Dig and delve;

Thirteen, fourteen,
Maids a-courting;

Fifteen, sixteen,
Maids in the kitchen;

Seventeen, eighteen,
Maids in waiting;

Nineteen, twenty,
My plate's empty.

HICKORY DICKORY DOCK

illustrated by
Toni Goffe

Hickory, dickory, dock,
The mouse ran up the clock.

The clock struck one,

The mouse ran down,
Hickory, dickory, dock.

Tick, tock, tick, tock, tick, tock.

TIME TO
LAUGH

RED FOX DANCES

by ALAN BARON

Red Fox was hungry. He was creeping through the woods, hunting for his dinner. Suddenly he heard something.

Red Fox crept towards the sound. He crouched behind a bush. He saw Little Pig dancing a jig. Ah, dinner! Red Fox licked his lips. But Dan Dog was there too, playing the fiddle. Red Fox watched and waited.

Along came Big Duck and Fat Hen. They began to dance a jig. Little Pig hopped and bopped. Dan Dog played faster. Behind the bush, Red Fox began to tap his toes.

Along came Tabby Cat and Lucy Goose. They began to dance a jig. Big Duck and Fat Hen hopped and bopped. Little Pig did a big twirl. Dan Dog played faster and faster. Behind the bush, Red Fox began to twitch.

46

Suddenly Red Fox jumped out.
"Call that dancing?"
he shouted.
"I'll show you how to dance!"
Everyone was terribly frightened.
But Dan Dog kept playing
so everyone kept dancing.

Red Fox started to dance.

He rocked and rolled.

He skipped and jumped.

He did high kicks
and big leaps.

He bounced and
bounced and bounced.

Red Fox was so busy showing off he didn't notice everyone
was dancing away from him. He didn't notice the music growing
fainter and fainter.

Suddenly Red Fox remembered he was hungry.
He stopped dancing and looked around.
"WHERE'S MY DINNER?"
he howled. But there was no
answer. Red Fox's dinner
had danced away.

"Quack!" said the

"Quack!" said the billy-goat.

"Oink!" said the hen.

"Miaow!" said the little chick

running in the pen.

"Hobble-gobble!" said the dog.

"Cluck!" said the sow.

"Tu-whit tu-whoo!" the donkey said.

"Baa!" said the cow.

"Hee-haw!" the turkey cried.

The duck began to moo.

All at once the sheep went,

"Cock-a-doodle-doo!"

The owl coughed and

cleared his throat

and he began to bleat.

"Bow-wow!" said the cock

swimming in the leat.

"Cheep-cheep!" said the cat

as she began to fly.

48

billy-goat

by Charles Causley
illustrated by Barbara Firth

"Farmer's been and laid an egg –
that's the reason why."

"ONLY JOKING!"
LAUGHED THE LOBSTER
BY COLIN WEST

"Look out, Fish, there's a
shark following you!
... only joking!"
laughed the lobster.

"Look out, Eel,
there's a great big
shark following you!
... only joking!" laughed the lobster.

"Look out, Crab, there's a great
big ugly shark following you!
... only joking!" laughed the lobster.

"Look out, Turtle, there's a great big
ugly wild-looking shark following you!
... only joking!" laughed the lobster.

"Look out, Octopus, there's a
great big ugly wild-looking
mean old shark following you!
... only joking!" laughed the lobster.

"Look out, Shark, there's a
great big ugly wild-looking
mean old hungry shark ..."

"SWALLOWING YOU!" said the shark.
And he wasn't joking!

A LIMERICK *by*

EDWARD LEAR

There was an Old Man on whose nose,

Most birds of the air could repose;

But they all flew away

At the closing of day,

Which relieved that Old Man and his nose.

illustrated by

EMMA CHICHESTER CLARK

TIME

TO BE
QUIET

One Summer Day

BY KIM LEWIS

One day Max saw a huge red tractor with a plough roar by.

"Go out," said Max, racing to find his shoes and coat and hat. He hurried back to the window and looked out.

Two boys walked along with fishing-rods. Max's friend Sara cycled past in the sun. Max pressed his nose to the window, but the tractor was gone.

As Max looked out, suddenly Sara looked in.

"Peekaboo!" she said.

Then Max heard a knock at the door. "Can Max come out?"

"It's a summer day," laughed Sara, helping Max take off his coat. The sun was hot and the grass smelled sweet. Max and Sara walked down the farm road.

Max and Sara stopped to watch the hens feeding. One hen pecked at Max's foot.

"Shoo!" cried Max and sent the hens flapping.

Max and Sara ran through a field where the grass was very high. A cow with her calf mooed loudly. Max made a small "Moo!" back.

Max and Sara came to the river.

"Look, the boys are fishing," said Sara.

Sara caught Max and took off his shoes before he ran in to paddle.

Then Max and Sara reached a gate. Sara sat Max on top. They heard a roar in the field coming nearer and louder.

"Tractor!" shouted Sara and Max.

Max clung to the gate as the tractor loomed past. It pulled a huge plough which

Sara carried Max back up the road.

"Tractor," sighed Max and closed his eyes.

Max woke up when they reached his house.

"Goodbye, Max," said Sara. "See you soon."

Max raced inside to the window. Sara looked in as Max looked out.

"Peepo!" said Max, and pressed his nose to the glass.

flashed in the sun. The field was full of gulls.

"Let's go home," said Sara to Max.

They walked beside the freshly ploughed field, along by the river and through the grass.

Danny's Duck

A duck flew over the land, looking for a good woody place. Down she flew to a pile of brushwood at the edge of a school playground. No one saw her come.
Except Danny.

At playtime he looked for her.
He had to look hard. Her colours were so like the colours of the twigs and branches.
But Danny saw her.
And she saw him.

by *June Crebbin* • illustrated by *Clara Vulliamy*

In school Danny drew the duck sitting.

"How lovely," said his teacher. "A duck on her nest."

When Danny visited the pile of brushwood again, the duck was still there, sitting very still. Again she saw him. Then she stood up and stretched.

Danny saw her eggs. He looked and counted.

In school he drew a picture of the nest with nine pale green eggs in it.

"How lovely," said his teacher. "They'll have ducklings inside, growing."

Danny visited the duck every day. Children played in the playground. Parents passed close by on the footpath. But no one saw.

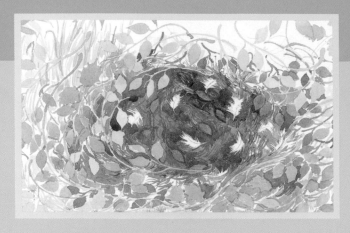

One sunny morning, just as he always did, Danny ran into the playground and over to the pile of brushwood.

But the duck wasn't there. Nor were her eggs. The nest was empty. Danny cried. He cried and cried.

In school he drew a picture of the empty nest. But when his teacher saw the picture – she smiled!

"The mother duck eats the egg-shells," she said, "after the eggs have hatched."

At lunch-time, Danny took his teacher across the playground to the pile of brushwood.

There was the nest.

Then his teacher took Danny
across the school field, to the pond.
Danny looked.
"There's my duck!" he shouted.
"And – one, two, three, four, five,
six, seven, eight, *nine ducklings!*"
And everyone came to see.

Rosie's Babies

by **Martin Waddell**

illustrated by **Penny Dale**

Mum was putting the baby to bed and Rosie said, "I've got two babies and you've only got one."
"Two, including you," said Mum.
"I'm not a baby, I'm four years old," said Rosie.
"Tell me about your babies," Mum said.

And Rosie said, "My babies live in a bird's nest and they are nearly as big as me. They go out in the garden all by themselves and sometimes they make me cross!"
"Do they?" said Mum.
"Yes, when they do silly things!" said Rosie.
"What silly things do they do?" asked Mum.

And Rosie said, "My babies climbed a big mountain. That was silly, because they couldn't get down. They jumped, and they bumped on their bottoms!"
"Silly babies," said Mum. "Did they hurt themselves?"

rockers and dinosaurs. They go to the park when it's dark and there are no mums and dads who can see, only me!"
"Gracious!" said Mum.
"Aren't they scared?"

And Rosie said,
"One of my babies hurt her knee. I bandaged it up and she cried and I said 'Never mind' because I am kind."
"I'm sure you are," said Mum.
"What else do your babies do?"

And Rosie said,
"My babies drive cars that are real ones and lorries and dumpers and boats. My babies are very good drivers."
"What do your babies like doing best?" asked Mum.

And Rosie said,
"My babies like swings and

And Rosie said,
"My babies are scared of the big dogs, but I'm not. I go GRRRRRRRRRR! and frighten the big dogs away."
"They are not very scared then?" said Mum.
"My babies know I will look after them," said Rosie.
"I'm their mum."
"How do you look after them?" Mum asked.

And Rosie said,
"I make their teas and I tell them stories and I take them for walks and I talk to them and I tell them that I love them."
"That's a good way to look after babies!" said Mum. "Do you make them nice things to eat, like pies?"

And Rosie said,
"My babies make their own pies, but they never eat them."
"What do they eat?" asked Mum.

And Rosie said,
"My babies eat apples and

And Rosie thought and thought and thought and then Rosie said,
"My babies have gone to bed."
"Just like this one," said Mum.
"I don't want to talk about my babies any more because they are asleep," said Rosie. "I don't want them to wake up, or they'll cry."
"We could talk very softly," said Mum.
"Yes," said Rosie.
"What will we talk about?" asked Mum.

And Rosie said,
"ME!"

apples and apples all the time. And grapes and pears but they don't like the pips."
"Most babies don't," said Mum.
"Are you going to tell me more about your babies?"

READING

by Jan Ormerod

climbing over
crawling under
looking through
pushing through
climbing up
relaxing
peeping over
reading

TIME TO
LOOK

by Dayle Ann Dodds

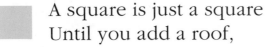 A square is just a square
Until you add a roof,
Two windows and a door –
Then it's much, much more!

A triangle's just a triangle
Until you add another,
An ocean and a sky,
A seagull passing by.

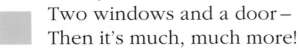 A circle's just a circle
Until you add some lights,
Chairs high and low –
Round and round they go.

A rectangle's just a rectangle
Until you add some more,
An engine and a track
And engine driver Jack.

OF THINGS ◆ ⬭ △

illustrated by Julie Lacome

An oval's just an oval
Until you add a nest,
A wooden house and then
A patient mother hen.

A diamond's just a diamond
Until you add some string,
Wind and a tail,
Some friends to help it sail.

A shape is just a shape, but look again and see ...
There are shapes of every kind! How many can you find?

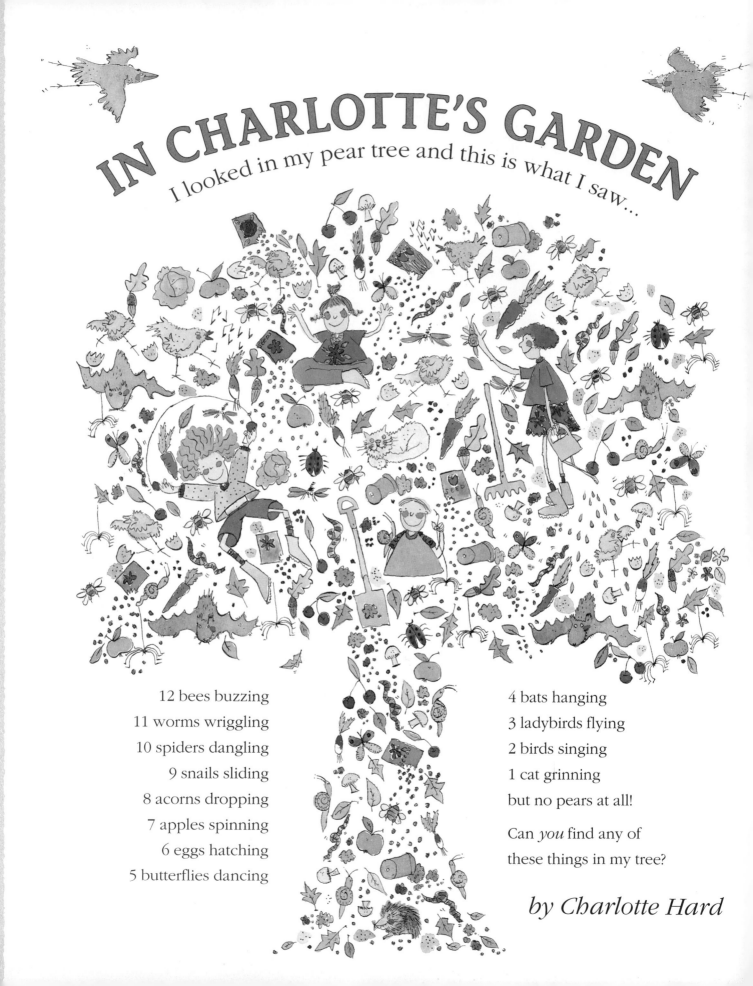

IN CHARLOTTE'S GARDEN

I looked in my pear tree and this is what I saw...

12 bees buzzing

11 worms wriggling

10 spiders dangling

9 snails sliding

8 acorns dropping

7 apples spinning

6 eggs hatching

5 butterflies dancing

4 bats hanging

3 ladybirds flying

2 birds singing

1 cat grinning

but no pears at all!

Can *you* find any of these things in my tree?

by Charlotte Hard

TIME TO · LISTEN

Daisy Dare

by Anita Jeram

Daisy Dare did things her friends were far too scared to do.

"Just dare me," she said. "Anything you like. I'm never, *ever* scared!"

So they dared her to walk the garden wall.

They dared her to eat a worm.

They dared her to stick out her tongue at Miss Crumb.
And she did!

One day, Daisy's friends thought of a really scary dare to do. They whispered it to Daisy.

"I'm not doing that!" she said.

"Daisy Dare-not!" they laughed.

Daisy took a deep breath. "All right," she said. "I'll do it."

This was the dare: to take the bell off the cat's collar.

The cat was asleep. That was good. The bell slipped off easily. That was good too. But Daisy's hands trembled so much that the bell tinkled, the cat woke up and that was very, very bad!

Daisy ran and ran as fast as she could, back to her friends, through the garden gate, and into the house where the cat couldn't follow.

"Phew!" said Billy.

"Wow!" gasped Joe.

"You're the bravest, most daring mouse in the whole world!" shouted Contrary Mary.

Daisy Dare grinned with pride.

"Just dare me," she said. "Anything you like… I'm only *sometimes* scared!"

TOM AND PIPPO GO FOR A WALK

by Helen Oxenbury

Mummy and I were going for a walk. Mummy said it was very cold outside and I must wear my hat, scarf and gloves.

Pippo wanted to
come for a walk too.

I made him put on
his hat and
scarf and I told him
he would
catch a
cold if
he didn't.

Mummy held Pippo
while I went for a
run down the hill.

Pippo wanted to run
with me, but we fell over.
I'm sure Pippo
made me run
too fast.

Mummy put me straight in the bath,
but Pippo had to go
in the basin.

Then Pippo and I sat
by the fire and had
a warm drink.

THE CRAB AND HIS MOTHER

ONE OF AESOP'S FABLES RETOLD BY MARGARET CLARK
ILLUSTRATED BY CHARLOTTE VOAKE

"*Why can't you walk properly?*" *complained a mother crab to her baby. "Stop walking sideways."*

"I'm only copying what you do," said the little crab. "If you show me how, I'll walk straight."

But the mother crab only knew how to walk sideways, as all crabs do, so the baby went on as before.

FOLLOW THE SNAIL TRAIL

The best place to look for snails is under a stone or log, where it is wet and cool. Snails like damp places. On hot, dry days, they hide away and only come out at night.

In the spring snails lay eggs in the soil. These take two to four weeks to hatch.

MY SNAIL TRAIL YOU WILL SEE WHERE THE SNAIL HAS BEEN!

LOOK UNDERNEATH A SNAIL AND YOU WILL SEE A LONG FLAT FOOT. THE SNAIL USES THIS TO MOVE ALONG. SLIME OOZES OUT OF THE FRONT OF THE SNAIL'S BODY TO HELP IT GLIDE SMOOTHLY. SNAILS CAN TRAVEL ALMOST ANYWHERE, EVEN UP WALLS! IF YOU FOLLOW THE GLISTENING, SLIPPE...

The snail carries a shell on its back for protection. If it is frightened, the snail quickly pulls its body into the shell until it is safe to come out again. The shell stays damp inside. In dry weather the snail shelters inside its shell to stop its soft body from drying out. It also shelters there during the coldest part of winter. The snail breathes in air through a small hole in its body, underneath the shell.

Gardeners don't like snails much. Snails eat leaves, stems and roots of plants by scraping them with their tongues which are covered with rows of tiny teeth.

CLOSED UNTIL SPRING

A snail has a long moist body with two pairs of tentacles on its head. At the end of the long pair are two eyes. The short pair is used to smell things.

Baby snails grow quickly. Soon they are so big they have to hide from birds that like snails for tea.

by Cecilia Fitzsimons
illustrated by Cecilia Fitzsimons
and Emma Boon

BEACH COMBING

SWISHY SWOSHY SPLASHY.

Pick up a seashell on the beach, and everything about it reminds you of the sea. It's swirly like water or smooth and round like a pebble. If it's hollow and you press it to your ear, you can hear the sound of the waves.

Every shell was once the home of a sea creature. The spiral shells you find belonged to creatures who glided around on one foot like snails...

SNAP!

Jellyfish can sting! Beware! Don't touch it!

Count the waves. Every seventh one will be a big one.

by BARBARA FIRTH
illustrated by DOM MANSELL

Around the rugged rocks the ragged rascal ran!

Say this tongue-twister ten times – very fast!

Then there are flatter shells that come in twos, joined by a hinge. Usually, you only find one half on its own. It might have belonged to a queen scallop, who flapped around the sea bed like a stone butterfly ... or to a long pod razor, who lay deep in the sand ... or to a mussel, who bound his shell to the rocks just above the tideline and waited for the sea to cover him.

But in the end, like all the other shells and pebbles on the shore, it will be washed and tumbled and broken by the tides until it becomes the sand you wiggle your toes in.

wiggle wriggle tickle

Next time you're on the beach, see if you can spot these shells:

COMMON WHELK

PERIWINKLE

LIMPET

QUEEN SCALLOP

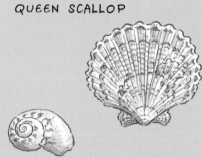

NECKLACE SHELL

MUSSEL

RAZOR SHELL

TOP-SHELL

STRAWBERRIES

by Phyllis King

Squatting down in a strawberry field is the way I like to eat strawberries.

Some people like them in a dish with cream and sugar, but I like them best warm and sweet with the sun, straight from the plant.

strawberry flower

At a strawberry farm you can pick your own, down on your knees. The best ones are often hidden under the leaves. While you fill your basket, you can fill your mouth too. And when you get home, you can help make strawberry jam.

BEDTIME

TEN IN THE BED

There were *ten* in
the bed and the little
one said,
"Roll over, roll over!"
So they all rolled over
and Hedgehog fell out ...

BUMP!

There were *nine* in
the bed and the little
one said,
"Roll over, roll over!"
So they all rolled over
and Zebra fell out ...

OUCH!

There were *eight* in
the bed and the little
one said,
"Roll over, roll over!"
So they all rolled over
and Ted fell out ...

THUMP!

There were *four* in the bed
and the little one said,
"Roll over, roll over!"
So they all rolled over
and Nelly fell out ...

CRASH!

There were *three* in the bed
and the little one said,
"Roll over, roll over!"
So they all rolled over
and Bear fell out ...

SLAM!

So they all came back
and jumped into bed –
Hedgehog, Mouse, Nelly, Zebra, Ted,
the little one, Rabbit, Croc, Bear and Sheep.
Ten in the bed, all fast asleep.

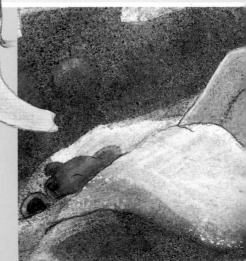

by Penny Dale

There were *seven* in the bed and the little one said,
"Roll over, roll over!"
So they all rolled over and Croc fell out ...

THUD!

There were *six* in the bed and the little one said,
"Roll over, roll over!"
So they all rolled over and Rabbit fell out ...

BONK!

There were *five* in the bed and the little one said,
"Roll over, roll over!"
So they all rolled over and Mouse fell out ...

DINK!

There were *two* in the bed and the little one said,
"Roll over, roll over!"
So they all rolled over and Sheep fell out ...

DONK!

There was *one* in the bed and the little one said,
"I'm cold!
I miss you!"

Can't You Sleep, Little Bear?

by Martin Waddell • *illustrated by Barbara Firth*

Once there were two bears. Big Bear and Little Bear. Big Bear is the big bear, and Little Bear is the little bear.

They played all day in the bright sunlight. When night came, and the sun went down, Big Bear took Little Bear home to the Bear Cave.

Big Bear put Little Bear to bed in the dark part of the cave.

"Go to sleep, Little Bear," he said.

And Little Bear tried.

Big Bear settled in the Bear Chair and read his Bear Book, by the light of the fire. But Little Bear couldn't get to sleep.

"Can't you sleep, Little Bear?" asked Big Bear, putting down his Bear Book (which was just getting to the interesting part) and padding over to the bed.

"I'm scared," said Little Bear.

"Why are you scared, Little Bear?" asked Big Bear.

"I don't like the dark," said Little Bear.

"What dark?" said Big Bear.

"The dark all around us," said Little Bear.

Big Bear looked, and he saw that the dark part of the cave was very dark, so he went to the Lantern Cupboard and took out the tiniest lantern that was there. Big Bear lit the tiniest lantern, and put it near to Little Bear's bed.

"There's a tiny light to stop you being scared, Little Bear," said Big Bear.

"Thank you, Big Bear," said Little Bear, cuddling up in the glow.

"Now go to sleep, Little Bear," said Big Bear, and he padded back to the Bear Chair and settled down to read the Bear Book, by the light of the fire.

Little Bear tried to go to sleep, but he couldn't.

"Can't you sleep, Little Bear?" yawned Big Bear, putting down his Bear Book (with just four pages to go to the interesting bit) and padding over to the bed.

"I'm scared," said Little Bear.

"Why are you scared, Little Bear?" asked Big Bear.

"I don't like the dark," said Little Bear.

"What dark?" asked Big Bear.

"The dark all around us," said Little Bear.

"But I brought you a lantern!" said Big Bear.

"Only a tiny-weeny one," said Little Bear. "And there's lots of dark!"

Big Bear looked, and he saw that Little Bear was quite right, there was still lots of dark. So Big Bear went to the Lantern Cupboard and took out a bigger lantern. Big Bear lit the lantern, and put it beside the other one.

"Now go to sleep, Little Bear," said Big Bear and he padded back to the Bear Chair and settled down to read the Bear Book, by the light of the fire.

Little Bear tried and tried to go to sleep, but he couldn't.

"Can't you sleep, Little Bear?" grunted Big Bear, putting down his Bear Book (with just three pages to go) and padding over to the bed.

"I'm scared," said Little Bear.

"Why are you scared, Little Bear?" asked Big Bear.

"I don't like the dark," said Little Bear.

"What dark?" asked Big Bear.

"The dark all around us," said Little Bear.

"But I brought you two lanterns!" said Big Bear. "A tiny one and a bigger one!"

"Not much bigger," said Little Bear. "And there's still lots of dark."

Big Bear thought about it, and then he went to the Lantern Cupboard and took out the Biggest Lantern of Them All, with two handles and a bit of chain. He hooked the lantern up above Little Bear's bed.

"I've brought you the Biggest Lantern of Them All!" he told Little Bear. "That's to stop you being scared!"

"Thank you, Big Bear," said Little Bear, curling up in the glow and watching the shadows dance.

"Now go to sleep, Little Bear," said Big Bear and he padded back to the Bear Chair and settled down to read the Bear Book, by the light of the fire.

Little Bear tried and tried and tried to go to sleep, but he couldn't.

"Can't you sleep, Little Bear?" groaned Big Bear, putting down his Bear Book (with just two pages to go) and padding over to the bed.

"I'm scared," said Little Bear.

"Why are you scared, Little Bear?" asked Big Bear.

"I don't like the dark," said Little Bear.

"What dark?" asked Big Bear.

"The dark all around us," said Little Bear.

"But I brought you the Biggest Lantern of Them All, and there isn't any dark left," said Big Bear.

"Yes, there is!" said Little Bear. "There is, out there!" And he pointed out of the Bear Cave, at the night.

Big Bear saw that Little Bear was right. Big Bear was very puzzled. All the lanterns in the world couldn't light up the dark outside.

Big Bear thought about it for a long time, and then he said, "Come on, Little Bear."

"Where are we going?" asked Little Bear.

"Out!" said Big Bear.

"Out into the darkness?" said Little Bear.

"Yes!" said Big Bear.

"But I'm scared of the dark!" said Little Bear.

"No need to be!" said Big Bear, and he took Little Bear by the paw and led him out from the cave into the night and it was … DARK!

"Ooooh! I'm scared," said Little Bear, cuddling up to Big Bear. Big Bear lifted Little Bear, and cuddled him, and said, "Look at the dark, Little Bear." And Little Bear looked.

"I've brought you the moon, Little Bear," said Big Bear. "The bright yellow moon, and all the twinkly stars."

But Little Bear didn't say anything, for he had gone to sleep, warm and safe in Big Bear's arms.

Big Bear carried Little Bear back into the Bear Cave, fast asleep and he settled down with Little Bear on one arm and the Bear Book on the other, cosy in the Bear Chair by the fire.

And Big Bear read the Bear Book right to …

THE END